The Christmas Tree

Paradise Press, Inc.

A family of field mice were getting ready for Christmas. The youngest mouse named Sam wanted to decorate the big fir tree that practically touched the sky.

But Father Mouse was worried. "If we put up decorations," he insisted, "the bigger animals will notice us and we'll be Christmas dinner!"

"But father," Sam began, "Christmas is a time for friendship and getting along."

"Yes, son," his father said. "I know what you mean. But the other animals may not agree with you."

The children were very disappointed.

"There must be a way to have Christmas all together," Sam insisted. "I know! What if we make friends with the other animals and invite them to join us for Christmas."

His father just laughed. "Impossible," he cried. "What foolishness! Imagine sharing Christmas with all the large, hungry animals in the woods!"

But Mrs. Mouse thought it was a good idea.

"You never know, dear," she said. "After all, Christmas is a magical time. I think if our little ones have some ideas about how to do this, we should let them try—as long as they don't put themselves in danger."

So Sam and Emily, his sister, got busy making invitations. "We'll invite all the animals to a meeting on Christmas eve," Sam explained. "Then we'll see if everyone will pitch in and cooperate."

And that's just what the little mice did.

When the invitations were ready, they delivered them in person to the birds, raccoons, skunks, squirrels, woodchucks, possums, and even the old red fox. Of course they made sure that the animals were off drinking at the stream and it was safe.

"This is going to the best Christmas in the woods," Sam said happily.

"But, Sam," Emily replied, "what if nobody wants to have Christmas with us?"

"Just leave everything to me," said Sam.

On Christmas eve, the mice stayed in the branches of the big fir tree and spoke to everyone who waited down below.

"Will you share in our Christmas celebration?" Sam asked. "That means being good and kind to all the smaller creatures in the woods. Then we can have a great party and eat together and be together and sing together and play together!"

The raccoons, squirrels, possums, skunks, woodchucks, and birds all agreed to spend Christmas together in peace and harmony. Even the sly, old fox nodded in agreement.

"What shall we do first?" asked Mrs. Possum.

"Well," said Emily, "We could use some help decorating the big fir tree."

So all the animals got busy making bows, and twig ornaments, and stringing cranberries.

And they were so happy, they sang as they worked:

"Oh, together we'll make the woods a special place
and decorate our very own Christmas tree!
It's fun to work together and all get along,
'Cause Christmas is coming for you and for me!"

Mr. and Mrs. Mouse made pies and dandelion stew from the greens and berries they could gather.

The squirrels shared their large stash of nuts they had been storing.

Everybody was busy pitching in except for the fox.

"Christmas—bah humbug!" the fox snarled, watching all the activity around him. "I know what I want for Christmas! Some plump juicy field mice!"

And while Emily Mouse was busy tying bows on a little wreath, the crafty old fox put a paw on the end of her tail. Then he slowly pulled her towards him. Poor Emily never even knew what was happening.

Luckily Mrs. Mouse was nearby. Outraged, she grabbed a large twig and hit the fox right on his long pointy nose.

"Ouch!" cried the fox. He quickly let go of Emily's tail to rub his nose with his paws.

"Aren't you ashamed of yourself!" cried Mrs. Mouse, waving the twig in the air. "Where is your Christmas spirit?"

"Oh, poor fox," said Emily, running over to him. "Let me see your nose. Why, this nice cool leaf will take the sting away."

The fox was so grateful to little Emily for wanting to help him, that he lost his appetite for mice right on the spot. He decided to join in this special Christmas in the woods.

After that little episode, everyone got along very well. The animals in the woods had a wonderful Christmas celebration under the most beautiful Christmas tree ever!